THE SEVEN
SINDBAD
SAILOR

TRANSLATED BY N. J. DAWOOD

PENGUIN BOOKS

PENGUIN BOOKS

Published by the Penguin Group. Penguin Books Ltd, 27 Wrights Lane, London w8 5tz, England. Penguin Books USA Inc., 375 Hudson Street, New York, New York 10014, USA. Penguin Books Australia Ltd, Ringwood, Victoria, Australia. Penguin Books Canada Ltd, 10 Alcorn Avenue, Toronto, Ontario, Canada m4v 3b2. Penguin Books (NZ) Ltd, 182–190 Wairau Road, Auckland 10, New Zealand · Penguin Books Ltd, Registered Offices: Harmondsworth, Middlesex, England · **These stories are taken from *Tales from the Thousand and One Nights*, translated by N. J. Dawood and published by Penguin Books in 1973.** This edition published 1995 · Translation copyright 1954 by N. J. Dawood. Translation copyright © N. J. Dawood, 1973. All rights reserved · Typeset by Datix International Limited, Bungay, Suffolk. Printed in England by Clays Ltd, St Ives plc · Except in the United States of America, this book is sold subject to the condition that it shall not, by way of trade or otherwise, be lent, re-sold, hired out, or otherwise circulated without the publisher's prior consent in any form of binding or cover other than that in which it is published and without a similar condition including this condition being imposed on the subsequent purchaser · 10 9 8 7 6 5 4 3 2 1

Once upon a time, in the reign of the Caliph Haroun al-Rashid, there lived in the city of Baghdad a poor man who earned his living by carrying burdens upon his head. He was called Sindbad the Porter.

One day, as he was staggering under a heavy load in the sweltering heat of the summer sun, he passed by a merchant's house that stood in a pleasant, shaded spot on the roadside. The ground before it was well swept and watered; and Sindbad, seeing a broad wooden bench just outside the gates, put down his load and sat there to rest awhile and to wipe away the sweat which trickled down his forehead. A cool and fragrant breeze blew through the doorway, and from within came the melodious strains of the lute and voices singing. They mingled with the choirs of birds warbling hymns to Allah in various tongues and tunes: curlews and pigeons, merles and bulbuls and turtle-doves.

Moved with great joy, he went up to the door and, looking within, saw in the centre of the noble courtyard a beautiful garden, around which stood numerous slaves and eunuchs and such an array of attendants as can be found only in the courts of illustrious kings. And all about the place floated the aroma of the choicest meats and wines.

Still marvelling at the splendour of what he saw, Sindbad lifted up his burden and was about to go his way when there came from within a handsome and well-dressed little page, who took him by the hand, saying: 'Pray come in; my master wishes to speak with you.'

The porter politely declined; but the lad would take no refusal. So Sindbad left his burden in the vestibule with the door-keeper and followed the page into the house.

He was conducted into a magnificent and spacious hall, where an impressive company of nobles and mighty sheikhs were seated according to rank at tables spread with the daintiest meats and richest wines, and gaily decked with flowers and fruit. On one side of the hall sat beautiful slave-girls who sang and made music; and to the fore reclined the host, a venerable old man whose beard was touched with silver. Bewildered at the grandeur and majesty of all that he beheld, the porter thought to himself: 'By Allah, this must either be a corner of Paradise or the palace of some mighty king!'

Sindbad courteously greeted the distinguished assembly and, kissing the ground before them, wished them joy and prosperity. He then stood in silence with eyes cast down.

The master of the house welcomed him kindly and bade him draw near and be seated. He ordered his slaves to set before the porter a choice of delicate foods and pressed him to eat. After pronouncing the blessing Sindbad fell to, and when he had eaten his fill washed his hands and thanked the old sheikh for his hospitality.

'You are welcome to this house, my friend,' said the host, 'and may this day bring you joy. We would gladly know your name and calling.'

'My name is Sindbad,' he answered, 'by trade a porter.'

'How strange a chance!' smiled the old man. 'For my name, too, is Sindbad. They call me Sindbad the Sailor, and marvel at my strange history. Presently, my brother, you shall hear the tale of my fortunes and all the hardships that I suffered before I rose to my present state and became the lord of this mansion where we are now assembled. For only after long toil, fearful ordeals, and dire peril did I achieve this fame. Seven voyages I made in all, each a story of such marvel as confounds the reason and fills the soul with wonder. All that befell me had been pre-ordained; and that which the moving hand of Fate has written no mortal power can revoke.'

The First Voyage of Sindbad the Sailor

Know, my friends, that my father was the chief merchant of this city and one of its richest men. He died whilst I was still a child, leaving me great wealth and many estates and farmlands. As soon as I came of age and had control of my inheritance, I took to extravagant living. I clad myself in the costliest robes, ate and drank sumptuously, and consorted with reckless prodigals of my own age, thinking that this mode of life would endure for ever.

It was not long before I awoke from my heedless folly to find that I had frittered away my entire fortune. I was stricken with horror and dismay at the gravity of my plight, and bethought myself of a proverb of our master Solomon son of David (may peace be upon them both!) which my father often used to cite: 'The day of death is better than the day of birth, a live dog is better than a dead lion, and the grave is better than poverty.' I sold the remainder of my lands and my household chattels for the sum of three thousand dirhams, and, fortifying myself with hope and courage, resolved to travel abroad and trade in foreign lands.

I bought a large quantity of merchandise and made preparations for a long voyage. Then I set sail together with a company of merchants in a river-ship bound for Basrah. There we put to sea and, voyaging many days and nights from isle to isle and from shore to shore, buying and selling and bartering wherever the ship anchored, we came at length to a little island as fair as the Garden of Eden. Here the captain of our ship cast anchor and put out the landing-planks.

The passengers went ashore and set to work to light a fire. Some busied themselves with cooking and washing, some fell to eating and drinking and making merry, while others, like myself, set out to explore the island. Whilst we were thus engaged we suddenly heard the captain cry out to us from the ship: 'All aboard, quickly! Abandon everything and run for your lives! The mercy of Allah be upon you, for this is no island but a gigantic whale floating on the bosom of the sea, on whose back the sands have settled and trees have grown since the world was young! When you lit the fire it felt the heat and stirred. Make haste, I say; or soon the whale will plunge into the sea and you will all be lost!'

Hearing the captain's cries, the passengers made for the ship in panic-stricken flight, leaving behind their cooking-pots and other belongings. Some reached the ship in safety, but others did not; for suddenly the island shook beneath our feet and, submerged by mountainous waves, sank with all that stood upon it to the bottom of the roaring ocean.

Together with my unfortunate companions I was engulfed by the merciless tide; but Providence came to my aid, casting in my way a great wooden trough which had been used by the ship's company for washing. Impelled by that instinct which makes all mortals cling to life, I held fast to the trough and, bestriding it firmly, paddled away with my feet as the waves tossed and buffeted me on every side. Meanwhile the captain hoisted sail and set off with the other passengers. I followed the ship with my eyes until it vanished from sight, and I resigned myself to certain death.

Darkness soon closed in upon the ocean. All that night and throughout the following day I drifted on, lashed by the wind and the waves, until the trough brought me to the steep shores of a densely wooded island, where trees hung over the sea.

5

I caught hold of one of the branches and with its aid managed to clamber ashore after fighting so long for my life. Finding myself again on dry land, I realized that I had lost the use of my legs, and my feet began to smart with the bites of fish.

Worn out by anguish and exertion, I sank into a death-like slumber; and it was not until the following morning when the sun rose that I came to my senses. But my feet were so sore and swollen that I could move about only by crawling on my knees. By good fortune, however, the island had an abundance of fruit-trees, which provided me with sustenance, and many springs of fresh water, so that after a few days my body was restored to strength and my spirit revived. I cut myself a staff from the branch of a tree, and with its aid set out to explore the island and to admire the many goodly things which Allah had planted on its soil.

One day, as I was roaming about the beach in an unfamiliar part of the island, I caught sight of a strange object in the distance which appeared to be some wild beast or sea-monster. As I drew nearer and looked more closely at it, I saw that it was a noble mare of an uncommonly high stature haltered to a tree. On seeing me the mare gave an ear-splitting neigh which made me take to my heels in terror. Presently a man emerged from the ground and pursued me, shouting: 'Who are you and whence have you come? What are you doing here?'

'Sir,' I replied, 'I am a luckless voyager, abandoned in the middle of the sea; but it was Allah's will that I should be rescued from the fury of the waves and cast upon this island.'

The stranger took me by the hand and bade me follow him. He led me to a subterranean cavern and, after asking me to be seated, he placed some food before me and invited me to eat.

When I had eaten my fill he questioned me about the fortunes of my voyage, and I related to him all that had befallen me from first to last.

'But, pray tell me, sir,' I inquired, as my host marvelled at my adventure, 'what is the reason of your vigil here and for what purpose is this mare tethered on the beach?'

'Know,' he replied, 'that I am one of the many grooms of King Mahrajan. We have charge of all his horses and are stationed in different parts of this island. Each month, on the night of the full moon, we tether all the virgin mares on the beach and hide in shelters near by. Presently the sea-horses scent the mares and, after emerging from the water, leap upon the beasts and cover them. Then they try to drag them away into the sea. But this they fail to do, as the mares are securely roped. With angry cries the sea-horses attack the mares and kick them with their hind legs. At this point we rush from our hiding-places and drive the sea-horses back into the water. The mares then conceive and bear colts and fillies of inestimable worth. Tonight,' he added, 'when we have completed our task, I shall take you to our King and show you our city. Allah be praised for this happy encounter; for had you not chanced to meet us you would have surely come to grief in the solitude of these wild regions.'

I thanked him with all my heart and called down blessings upon him. Whilst we were thus engaged in conversation we heard a dreadful cry in the distance. The groom quickly snatched up his sword and buckler and rushed out, shouting aloud and banging his sword on his shield. Thereupon several other grooms came out from their hiding-places, brandishing their spears and yelling at the top of their voices. The sea-horse, who had just covered the mare, took fright at this tumult and plunged, like a buffalo, headlong into the sea, where he disappeared beneath the water.

As we sat on the ground to recover our breath, the other grooms, each leading a mare, approached us. My companion explained to them the circumstances of my presence, and, after exchanging greetings, we rode to the city of King Mahrajan.

As soon as the King was informed of my arrival he summoned me to his presence. He marvelled at my story, saying: 'By Allah, my son, your preservation has been truly miraculous. Praise be to the Highest for your deliverance!'

Thenceforth I rose rapidly in the King's favour and soon became a trusted courtier. He vested me with robes of honour and appointed me Comptroller of Shipping at the port of his kingdom. And during my sojourn in that realm I earned the gratitude of the poor and the humble for my readiness to intercede for them with the King.

There I witnessed many prodigies and met travellers from different foreign lands. One day I entered the King's chamber and found him entertaining a company of Indians. I exchanged greetings with them and questioned them about their country. In the course of conversation I was astonished to learn that there were no fewer than seventy-two different castes in India. The noblest of these castes is known as Shakiriyah, and its members are renowned for piety and fair dealing. Another caste are the Brahmins. They are skilled breeders of camels, horses, and cattle, and, though they abstain from wine, they are a merry and pleasure-loving people.

Not far from the King's dominions there is a little island where at night is heard a mysterious beating of drums and clash of tambourines. Travellers and men from neighbouring isles told me that its inhabitants were a shrewd and diligent race.

In those distant seas I once saw a fish two hundred cubits in length, and another with a head that resembled an owl's. This I saw with my own eyes, and many other things no less strange and wondrous.

Whenever I walked along the quay I talked with the sailors and travellers from far countries, inquiring whether any of them had heard tell of the city of Baghdad and how far off it lay; for I never lost hope that I should one day find my way back to my native land. But there was none who knew of that city; and as the days dragged by, my longing for home weighed heavy upon my heart.

One day, however, as I stood on the wharf, leaning upon my staff and gazing out to sea, a ship bearing a large company of merchants came sailing into the harbour. As soon as it was moored, the sails were furled and landing-planks put out. The crew began to unload the cargo, and I stood by entering up the merchandise in my register. When they had done, I asked the captain if all the goods had now been brought ashore.

'Sir,' he replied, 'in the ship's hold I still have a few bales which belonged to a merchant who was drowned at an early stage of our voyage. We shall put them up for sale and take the money to his kinsmen in Baghdad, the City of Peace.'

'What was the merchant's name?' I demanded.

'Sindbad,' he answered.

I looked more closely into his face, and, recognizing him at once, uttered a joyful cry.

'Why!' I exclaimed, 'I am Sindbad, the self-same owner of these goods, who was left to drown with many others when the great whale plunged into the sea. But through the grace of Allah I was cast by the waves onto the shores of this island, where I found favour with the King and became Comptroller at this port. I am the true owner of these goods, which are my only possessions in this world.'

'By Allah,' cried the captain, 'is there no longer any faith or honesty in man? I have but to mention a dead man's goods and you claim them for your own! Why, we saw Sindbad drown before our very eyes. Dare you lay claim to his property?'

'I pray you, captain,' I rejoined, 'listen to my story and you shall soon learn the whole truth.' I then recounted to him all the details of the voyage from the day we set sail from Basrah till we cast anchor off the treacherous island and reminded him of a certain matter that had passed between us.

The captain and the passengers now recognized me, and all congratulated me on my escape, saying: 'Allah has granted you a fresh span of life!'

At once my goods were brought ashore and I rejoiced to find the bales intact and sealed as I had left them. I selected some of the choicest and most precious articles as presents for King Mahrajan, and had them carried by the sailors to the royal palace, where I laid them at his feet. I informed the King of the unexpected arrival of my ship and the happy recovery of all my goods. He marvelled greatly at this chance, and, in return for my presents, bestowed upon me priceless treasures.

I sold my wares at a substantial profit and re-equipped myself with the finest produce of that island. When all was ready for the homeward voyage I presented myself at the King's court, and, thanking him for the many favours he had shown me, begged leave to return to my land and people.

Then we set sail, trusting in Allah and propitious Fortune; and after voyaging many days and nights we at length arrived safely in Basrah.

I spent but a few days in that town and then, loaded with

treasure, set out for Baghdad, the City of Peace. I was overjoyed to be back in my native city, and hastening to my old street entered my own house, where by and by all my friends and kinsmen came to greet me.

I bought fine houses and rich farm-lands, concubines and eunuchs and black slaves, and became richer than I had ever been before. I kept open house for my old companions, and, soon forgetting the hardships of my voyage, resumed with new zest my former mode of living.

That is the story of the first of my adventures. Tomorrow, if Allah wills, I shall relate to you the tale of my second voyage.

The day was drawing to its close, and Sindbad the Sailor invited Sindbad the Porter to join the guests in the evening meal. When the feast was finished he gave him a hundred pieces of gold, saying: 'You have delighted us with your company this day.'

The porter thanked him for his generous gift and departed, pondering over the vicissitudes of fortune and marvelling at all that he had heard.

Next morning he went again to the house of his benefactor, who received him courteously and seated him by his side. Presently the other guests arrived, and when they had feasted and made merry, Sindbad the Sailor began:

The Second Voyage of Sindbad the Sailor

For some time after my return to Baghdad I continued to lead a joyful and carefree life, but it was not long before I felt an irresistible longing to travel again about the world and to visit distant cities and islands in quest of profit and adventure. So I bought a great store of merchandise and, after making preparations for departure, sailed down the Tigris to Basrah. There I embarked, together with a band of merchants, in a fine new vessel, well-equipped and manned by a sturdy crew, which set sail the same day.

Aided by a favourable wind, we voyaged for many days and nights from port to port and from island to island, selling and bartering our goods, and haggling with merchants and officials wherever we cast anchor. At length Destiny carried our ship to the shores of an uninhabited island, rich in fruit and flowers, and jubilant with the singing of birds and the murmur of crystal streams.

Here passengers and crew went ashore, and we all set off to enjoy the delights of the island. I strolled through the green meadows, leaving my companions far behind, and sat down in a shady thicket to eat a simple meal by a spring of water. Lulled by the soft and fragrant breeze which blew around me, I lay upon the grass and presently fell asleep.

I cannot tell how long I slept, but when I awoke I saw none of my fellow-travellers, and soon realized that the ship had sailed away without anyone noticing my absence. I ran in frantic haste towards the sea, and on reaching the shore saw the vessel, a white speck upon the vast blue ocean, dissolving into the far horizon.

Broken with terror and despair, I threw myself upon the sand, wailing: 'Now your end has come, Sindbad! The jar that drops a second time is sure to break!' I cursed the day I bade farewell to the joys of a contented life and bitterly repented my folly in venturing again upon the hazards and hardships of the sea, after having so narrowly escaped death in my first voyage.

At length, resigning myself to my doom, I rose and, after wandering about aimlessly for some time, climbed into a tall tree. From its top I gazed long in all directions, but could see nothing save the sky, the trees, the birds, the sands, and the boundless ocean. As I scanned the interior of the island more closely, however, I gradually became aware of some white object looming in the distance. At once I climbed down the tree and made my way towards it. Drawing nearer, I found to my astonishment that it was a white dome of extraordinary dimensions. I walked all round it, but could find no door or entrance of any kind; and so smooth and slippery was its surface that any attempt to climb it would have been fruitless. I walked round it again, and, making a mark in the sand near its base, found that its circumference measured more than fifty paces.

Whilst I was thus engaged the sun was suddenly hidden from my view as by a great cloud and the world grew dark around me. I lifted up my eyes towards the sky, and was confounded to see a gigantic bird with enormous wings which, as it flew through the air, screened the sun and hid it from the island.

The sight of this prodigy instantly called to my mind a story I had heard in my youth from pilgrims and adventurers – how in a far island dwelt a bird of monstrous size called the roc, which fed its young on elephants; and at once I realized that the white dome was no other than a roc's egg. In a twinkling the bird alighted upon the egg, covering it completely with its wings and stretching out its legs behind it on the ground. And in this posture it went to sleep. (Glory to Him who never sleeps!)

Rising swiftly, I unwound my turban from my head, then doubled it and twisted it into a rope with which I securely bound myself by the waist to one of the great talons of the monster. 'Perchance this bird,' I thought, 'will carry me away to a civilized land; wherever I am set down, it will surely be better than a solitary island.'

I lay awake all night, fearing to close my eyes lest the bird should fly away with me while I slept. At daybreak the roc rose from the egg, and, spreading its wings, took to the air with a terrible cry. I clung fast to its talon as it winged its flight through the void and soared higher and higher until it almost touched the heavens. After some time it began to drop, and sailing swiftly downwards came to earth on the brow of a steep hill.

Trembling with fear, I hastened to untie my turban before the roc became aware of my presence. Scarcely had I released myself when the monster darted off towards a great black object lying near and, clutching it in its fearful claws, took wing again. As it rose in the air I was astonished to see that this was a serpent of immeasurable length; and with its prey the bird vanished from sight.

Looking around, I found myself on a precipitous hillside overlooking an exceedingly deep and vast valley. On all sides towered craggy mountains whose beetling summits no man could ever scale. I was stricken with fear and repented my rashness. 'Would I had remained in that island!' I thought to myself. 'There at least I lacked neither fruit nor water, while these barren steeps offer nothing to eat or drink. No sooner do I escape from one peril than I find myself in another more grievous. There is no strength or help save in Allah!'

When I had made my way down the hill I marvelled to see the ground thickly covered with the rarest diamonds, so that the entire valley blazed with a glorious light. Here and there among the glittering stones, however, coiled deadly snakes and vipers, dread keepers of the fabulous treasure. Thicker and longer than giant palm-trees, they could have swallowed whole elephants at one gulp. They were crawling back into their sunless dens, for by day they hid themselves from their enemies the rocs and the eagles and moved about only at night.

Overwhelmed with horror, and oblivious of hunger and fatigue, I roamed the valley all day searching with infinite caution for a shelter where I might pass the night. At dusk I came upon a narrow-mouthed cave, into which I crawled, blocking its entrance from within by a great stone. I thought to myself: 'Here I shall be safe tonight. When tomorrow comes, let Destiny do its worst.'

Scarcely had I advanced a few steps, when I saw at the far end of the cave an enormous serpent coiled in a great knot round its eggs. My hair stood on end and I was transfixed with terror. Seeing no way of escape, however, I put my trust in Allah and kept vigil all night. At day break I rolled back the stone and staggered out of the cave, reeling like a drunken man.

As I thus stumbled along I noticed a great joint of flesh come tumbling down into the valley from rock to rock. Upon closer inspection I found this to be a whole sheep, skinned and drawn. I was deeply perplexed at the mystery, for there was not a soul in sight; but at that very moment there flashed across my mind the memory of a story I had once heard from travellers who had

15

visited the Diamond Mountains – how men obtained the diamonds from this treacherous and inaccessible valley by a strange device. Before sunrise they would throw whole carcasses of sheep from the top of the mountains, so that the gems on which they fell penetrated the soft flesh and became embedded in it. At midday rocs and mighty vultures would swoop down upon the mutton and carry it away in their talons to their nests in the mountain heights. With a great clamour the merchants would then rush at the birds and force them to drop the meat and fly away, after which it would only remain to look through the carcasses and pick out the diamonds.

As I recalled this story a plan of escape formed in my mind. I selected a great quantity of priceless stones and hid them all about me, filling my pockets with them and pressing them into the folds of my belt and garments. Then I unrolled my turban, stuffed it with more diamonds, twisted it into a rope as I had done before, and, lying down below the carcass, bound it firmly to my chest. I had not remained long in that position when I suddenly felt myself lifted from the ground by the talons of a huge vulture which had tightly closed upon the meat. The bird climbed higher and higher and finally alighted upon the top of a mountain. As soon as it began to tear at the flesh there arose from behind the neighbouring rocks a great tumult, at which the bird took fright and flew away. At once I freed myself and sprang to my feet, with face and clothes all bloody.

I saw a man come running to the spot and stop in alarm as he saw me. Without uttering a word he cautiously bent over the carcass to examine it, eyeing me suspiciously all the while; but finding no diamonds, he wrung his hands and lifted up his arms, crying: 'O heavy loss! Allah, in whom alone dwell all power and majesty, defend us from the wiles of the Evil One!'

Before I could explain my presence the man, shaking with fear, turned to me and asked: 'Who are you, and how came you here?'

'Do not be alarmed, sir,' I replied, 'I am no evil spirit, but an honest man, a merchant by profession. My story is an extraordinary one, and the adventure which has brought me to these mountains surpasses in wonder all the marvels that men have seen or heard of. But first pray accept some of these diamonds, which I myself gathered in the fearful valley below.'

I took some splendid jewels from my pocket and offered them to him, saying: 'These will bring you all the riches you can desire.'

The owner of the bait was overjoyed at the unexpected gift; he warmly thanked me and called down blessings upon me. Whilst we were thus talking, several other merchants came up from the mountain-side. They crowded round us, listening in amazement to my story, and congratulated me, saying: 'By Allah, your escape was a miracle; for no man has ever set foot in that valley and returned alive. Allah alone be praised for your salvation.'

The merchants then led me to their tent. They gave me food and drink and there I slept soundly for many hours. Early next day we set out from our tent and, after journeying over a vast range of mountains, came at length to the seashore. After a short voyage we arrived in a pleasant, densely wooded island, covered with trees so huge that beneath one of them a hundred men could shelter from the sun. It is from these trees that the aromatic substance known as camphor is extracted. The trunks are hollowed out, and the sap oozes drop by drop into vessels which are placed beneath, soon curdling into a crystal gum.

In that island I saw a gigantic beast called the karkadan, or rhinoceros, which grazes in the fields like a cow or buffalo. Taller than a camel, it has a single horn in the middle of its forehead, and upon this horn Nature has carved the likeness of a man. The karkadan attacks the elephant and, impaling it upon its horn, carries it aloft from place to place until its victim dies. Before long, however, the elephant's fat melts in the heat of the sun and, dripping down into the karkadan's eyes, puts out its sight, so that the beast blunders helplessly along and finally drops dead. Then the roc swoops down upon both animals and carries them off to its nest in the high mountains. I also saw many strange breeds of buffalo in that island.

I sold a part of my diamonds for a large sum and exchanged more for a vast quantity of merchandise. Then we set sail and, trading from port to port and from island to island, at length arrived safely in Basrah. After a few days' sojourn there I set out upstream to Baghdad, the City of Peace.

Loaded with precious goods and the finest of my diamonds, I hastened to my old street and, entering my own house, rejoiced to see my friends and kinsfolk. I gave them gold and presents, and distributed alms among the poor of the city.

I soon forgot the perils and hardships of my travels and took again to sumptuous living. I ate well, dressed well, and kept open house for innumerable gallants and boon companions.

From far and near men came to hear me speak of my adventures and to learn the news of foreign lands from me. All were astounded at the dangers I had escaped and wished me joy of my return. Such was my second voyage.

Tomorrow, my friends, if Allah wills, I shall relate to you the extraordinary tale of my third voyage.

The famous mariner ended. The guests marvelled at his story.

When the evening feast was over, Sindbad the Sailor gave Sindbad the Porter a hundred pieces of gold, which he took with thanks and many blessings, and departed, lost in wonderment at all he had heard.

Next day the porter rose and, after reciting his morning prayers, went to the house of his illustrious friend, who received him kindly and seated him by his side. And when all the guests had assembled, Sindbad the Sailor began:

The Third Voyage of Sindbad the Sailor

Know, my friends, that for some time after my return I continued to lead a happy and tranquil life, but I soon grew weary of my idle existence in Baghdad and once again longed to roam the world in quest of profit and adventure. Unmindful of the dangers of ambition and worldly greed, I resolved to set out on another voyage. I provided myself with a great store of goods and, after taking them down the Tigris, set sail from Basrah, together with a band of honest merchants.

The voyage began prosperously. We called at many foreign ports, trading profitably with our merchandise. One day, however, whilst we were sailing in mid ocean, we heard the captain of our ship, who was on deck scanning the horizon, suddenly burst out in a loud lament. He beat himself about the face, tore his beard, and rent his clothes.

'We are lost!' he cried, as we crowded round him. 'The treacherous wind has driven us off our course towards that island which you see before you. It is the Isle of the Zughb, where dwell a race of dwarfs more akin to apes than men, from whom no voyager has ever escaped alive!'

Scarcely had he uttered these words when a multitude of ape-like savages appeared on the beach and began to swim out towards the ship. In a few moments they were upon us, thick as a swarm of locusts. Barely four spans in height, they were the ugliest of living creatures, with little gleaming yellow eyes and bodies thickly covered with black fur. And so numerous were they that we did not dare to provoke them or attempt to drive them away, lest they should set upon us and kill us to a man by force of numbers.

They scrambled up the masts, gnawing the cables with their teeth and biting them to shreds. Then they seized the helm and steered the vessel to their island. When the ship had run ashore, the dwarfs carried us one by one to the beach, and, promptly pushing off again, climbed on board and sailed away.

Disconsolately we set out to search for food and water, and by good fortune came upon some fruit-trees and a running stream. Here we refreshed ourselves, and then wandered about the island until at length we saw far off among the trees a massive building, where we hoped to pass the night in safety. Drawing nearer, we found that it was a towering palace surrounded by a lofty wall, with a great ebony door which stood wide open. We entered the spacious courtyard, and to our surprise found it deserted. In one corner lay a great heap of bones, and on the far side we saw a broad bench, an open oven, pots and pans of enormous size, and many iron spits for roasting.

Exhausted and sick at heart, we lay down in the courtyard and were soon overcome by sleep. At sunset we were awakened by a noise like thunder. The earth shook beneath our feet and we saw a colossal black giant approaching from the doorway. He was a fearsome sight – tall as a palm-tree, with red eyes burning in his head like coals of fire; his mouth was a dark well, with lips that drooped like a camel's loosely over his chest, whilst his ears, like a pair of large round discs, hung back over his shoulders: his fangs were as long as the tusks of a boar and his nails were like the claws of a lion.

The sight of this monster struck terror to our hearts. We cowered motionless on the ground as we watched him stride across the yard and sit down on the bench. For a few moments he eyed us one by one in silence; then he rose and, reaching out towards me, lifted me up by the neck and began feeling my body as a butcher would a lamb. Finding me little more than skin and bone, however, he flung me to the ground and, picking up each of my companions in turn, pinched and prodded them and set them down until at last he came to the captain.

Now the captain was a corpulent fellow, tall and broad-shouldered. The giant seemed to like him well. He gripped him as a butcher grips a fatted ram and broke his neck under his foot. Then he thrust an iron spit through his body from mouth to backside and, lighting a great fire in the oven, carefully turned his victim round and round before it. When the flesh was finely roasted, the ogre tore the body to pieces with his fingernails as though it were a pullet, and devoured it limb by limb, gnawing the bones and flinging them against the wall. The monster then stretched himself out on the bench and soon fell fast asleep. His snores were as loud as the grunts and gurgles that issue from the throat of a slaughtered beast.

Thus he slept all night, and when morning came he rose and went out of the palace, leaving us half-crazed with terror.

As soon as we were certain that the monster had gone, we began lamenting our evil fortune. 'Would that we had been drowned in the sea or killed by the apes!' we cried. 'That would surely have been better than the foul death which now awaits us! But that which Allah has ordained must surely come to pass.'

We left the palace to search for some hiding-place, but could find no shelter in any part of the island, and had no choice but to return to the palace in the evening. Night came, and with it the black giant, announcing his approach by a noise like thunder. No sooner had he entered than he snatched up one of the merchants and prepared his supper in the same way as the night before. Then, stretching himself out to sleep, he snored the night away.

Next morning, when the giant had gone, we discussed our desperate plight.

'By Allah,' cried one of the merchants, 'let us rather throw ourselves into the sea than remain alive to be roasted and eaten!'

'Listen, my friends,' said another. 'We must kill this monster. For only by destroying him can we end his wickedness and save good Moslems from his barbarous cruelty.'

This proposal was received with general approbation; so I rose in my turn and addressed the company. 'If we are all agreed to kill this monster,' I said, 'let us first build a raft on which we can escape from this island as soon as we have sent his soul to damnation. Perchance our raft will take us to some other island, where we can board a ship bound for our country If we are drowned, we shall at least escape roasting and die a martyr's death.'

'By Allah,' cried the others, 'that is a wise plan.'

Setting to work at once, we hauled several logs from the great pile of wood stacked beside the oven and carried them out of the palace. Then we fastened them together into a raft, which we left ready on the seashore.

In the evening the earth shook beneath our feet as the black giant burst in upon us, barking and snarling like a mad dog. Once more he seized upon the stoutest of my companions and prepared his meal. When he had eaten his fill, he stretched himself upon the bench as was his custom and soon fell fast asleep.

Noiselessly we now rose, took two of the great iron spits from the oven, and thrust them into the fire. As soon as they were red 23 hot we carried them over to the snoring monster and plunged their sharpened ends deep into his eyes, exerting our united weight from above to push them home. The giant gave a deafening shriek which filled our hearts with terror and cast us back on the ground many yards away. Totally blinded, he leapt up from the bench groping for us with outstretched hands, while we nimbly dodged his frantic clutches. In despair he felt his way to the ebony door and staggered out of the yard, groaning in agonies of pain.

Without losing a moment we made off towards the beach. As soon as we reached the water we launched our raft and jumped aboard; but scarcely had we rowed a few yards when we saw the blind savage running towards us, guided by a foul hag of his own kind. On reaching the shore they stood howling threats and curses at us for a while, and then caught up massive boulders and hurled them at our raft with stupendous force. Missile followed missile until all my companions, save two, were drowned; but we three who escaped soon contrived to paddle beyond the range of their fury.

Lashed by the waves, we drifted on in the open sea for a whole day and a whole night until we were cast upon the shore of another island. Half-dead with hunger and exhaustion, we threw ourselves upon the sand and fell asleep.

Next morning, when we awoke, we found ourselves encircled by a serpent of prodigious size, which lay about us in a knotted coil. Before we could move a limb the beast suddenly reared its head and, opening wide its deadly jaws, seized one of my companions and swallowed him to the shoulders, then it gulped him down entirely, and we heard his ribs crack in its belly. Presently, however, the serpent unwound its loathsome body and, heedless of my companion and myself, glided away, leaving us stricken with grief at the horrible fate of our comrade and amazed at our own narrow escape.

'By Allah,' we cried, 'we have fled from one form of death only to meet with another as hideous. How shall we now escape this serpent? There is no strength or help save in Allah!'

The warmth of the new-born day inspired us with fresh courage, and we struck inland to search for food and water. Before nightfall we climbed into a tall tree, and perched ourselves as best we could upon the topmost branches. But as soon as darkness fell we heard a fearful hissing and a noise of heavy movement on the ground; and in a twinkling the serpent had seized my friend and gulped him down, cracking all his bones in its belly. Then the vile creature slid down the tree and disappeared among the vegetation. That was the end of the last of my companions.

At daybreak I climbed down from my hiding-place. My first thought was to throw myself into the sea and thus end a life which had already endured more than its share of hardships and ordeals. But when I was on the point of putting my resolve into execution, my courage failed me; for life is very precious. I clung instinctively to the hope of a speedy rescue, and a plan to protect myself from the serpent began to form in my mind.

I collected some thick planks of wood and fastened them together into a coffin-shaped box, complete with lid. When evening came I shut myself in, shielded on all sides by the strong boards. By and by the snake approached and circled round me, writhing and squirming. All night long its dreadful hissing sounded in my ears, but with the approach of morning it turned away and vanished among the undergrowth.

When the sun rose I came out of my shelter and cautiously made my way across the island. As I reached the shore, what 25 should I see but a ship sailing far off upon the vast expanse of water!

At once I tore off a great branch from a tree, and, yelling at the top of my voice, waved it frantically above my head. The crew must have instantly observed my signal, for, to my great joy, the ship suddenly turned off its course and headed for the island.

When I came aboard the captain gave me clothes to cover my nakedness and offered me food and drink. Little by little I regained my strength, and after a few days of rest became my old self again. I rendered thanks to Allah for rescuing me from my ordeal, and soon my past sufferings were no more than half-forgotten dreams.

Aided by a prosperous wind, we voyaged many days and nights and at length came to the Isle of Salahitah. Here the captain cast anchor, and the merchants landed with their goods to trade with the people of the island. Whilst I was standing idly by, watching the busy scene, the captain of our ship came up to me, saying: 'Listen, my friend. You say you are a penniless stranger who has suffered much at sea. I will make you an offer which, I trust, will be greatly to your advantage A few years ago I carried in my ship a merchant who, alas, was left behind upon a desert island. No news has since been heard of him, and no one knows whether he is alive or dead. Take his goods and trade with them, and a share of the profit shall be yours. The remainder of the money I will take back to the merchant's family in Baghdad.'

I thanked the captain with all my heart. He ordered the crew to unload the merchandise and called the ship's clerk to enter up the bales in his register.

26   'Whose property are they?' inquired the clerk.

'The owner's name was Sindbad,' replied the captain. 'But henceforth they will be in charge of this passenger.'

A cry of astonishment escaped my lips and I at once recognized him as the captain of the ship in which I had sailed on my second voyage.

'Why!' I exclaimed. 'I am Sindbad, that very merchant who many years ago was left behind on the Island of the Roc. I fell asleep beside a spring and awoke to find that the ship had gone. The merchants who saw me on the Diamond Mountains and heard my adventure will bear witness that I am indeed Sindbad.'

On hearing mention of the Diamond Mountains, one of the merchants, who by this time had gathered round us, came forward and, peering closely into my face, suddenly turned to his friends, crying: 'By Allah, not one of you would believe the wonder which I once witnessed on the Diamond Mountains, when a man was carried up from the valley by a mighty vulture! This is he; Sindbad the Sailor, the very one who presented me with those rare diamonds!'

The captain questioned me about the contents of my bales, and I readily gave him a precise description. I also reminded him of a certain incident which had occurred in the course of our voyage. He now recognized me and, taking me in his arms, congratulated me, saying: 'Praise be to Him who has brought us together again and granted the restitution of all your goods!'

My merchandise was brought ashore, and I sold it forthwith at a substantial profit. Then we set sail and after a few days came to the land of Sind, where we also traded profitably.

In those Indian waters I witnessed many prodigies. I saw a sea-monster which resembled a cow and another with a head like a donkey's. I also saw a bird which hatches from a sea-shell and remains throughout its life floating on the water.

27

From Sind we set sail again and, after voyaging many days and nights, came at length with Allah's help to Basrah. I stayed there but a few days, and then voyaged upstream to Baghdad, where I was jubilantly welcomed by my friends and kinsmen. I bestowed alms upon the poor and gave generously to widows and orphans, for I had returned from this voyage richer than ever before.

Tomorrow, my friends, if Allah wills, I shall recount to you the tale of my fourth voyage, which you shall find even more extraordinary than the tales I have already related.

When the evening feast was ended, Sindbad the Sailor gave Sindbad the Porter a hundred pieces of gold, and the company took leave of their host and departed, marvelling at the wonders they had heard.

Next morning the porter returned, and when the other guests had assembled, Sindbad the Sailor began:

The Fourth Voyage of Sindbad the Sailor

The jovial and extravagant life which I led after my return did not cause me to forget the delights and benefits of travel in distant lands; and my thirst for seeing the world, despite the perils I had encountered, continued as violent as ever. My restless soul at length yielded to the call of the sea and, after making preparations for a long voyage, I set sail with merchandise from Basrah, together with some eminent merchants of that city.

Blessed with a favouring wind, we sped upon the foamy highways of the sea, trading from port to port and from island to island. One day, however, a howling gale suddenly sprang up in mid ocean, rolling against our ship massive waves as high as mountains. The captain at once ordered the crew to cast anchor, and we all fell on our knees in prayer and lamentation. A furious squall tore the sails to ribbons and snapped the mast in two; then a giant wave came hurtling down upon us from above, shattering our vessel and tossing us all into the raging sea.

With Allah's help, I clung fast to a floating beam, and bestriding it firmly, fought the downrush of the waves with those of my companions who had managed to reach it also. Now paddling with our hands and feet, now swept by wind and current, we were at length thrown, half-dead with cold and exhaustion, on the shore of an island.

We lay down upon the sand and fell asleep. Next morning we rose and, striking inland, came after a few hours in sight of a lofty building among the trees. As we drew nearer, a number of naked and wild-looking men emerged from the door, and without a word took hold of my companions and myself and led us into the building, where we saw their King seated upon a throne.

The King bade us sit down, and presently his servants set before us dishes of such meats as we had never seen before in all our lives. My famished companions ate ravenously; but my stomach revolted at the sight of this food and, in spite of my hunger, I could not eat a single mouthful. As things turned out, however, my abstinence saved my life. For as soon as they had swallowed a few morsels my comrades began to lose their intelligence and to act like gluttonous maniacs, so that after a few hours of incessant guzzling they were little better than savages.

Whilst my companions were thus feeding, the naked men brought in a vessel filled with a strange ointment, with which they anointed their victims' bodies. The change my companions suffered was astonishing; their eyes sank into their heads and their bellies grew horribly distended, so that the more they swelled the more insatiable their appetites became.

My horror at this spectacle knew no bounds, especially when I soon discovered that our captors were cannibals who fattened their victims in this way before slaughtering them. The King feasted every day on a roasted stranger; his men preferred their diet raw.

When my transformed companions had thus been robbed entirely of all their human faculties, they were committed to the charge of a herdsman, who led them out every day to pasture in the meadows. I myself was reduced to a shadow by hunger and fear and my skin shrivelled upon my bones. Therefore the savages lost all interest in me and no longer cared even to watch my movements.

One day I slipped out of my captors' dwelling and made off
across the island. On reaching the distant grasslands I met the

herdsman with his once-human charges. But instead of pursuing me or ordering me to return he appeared to take pity on my helpless condition, and pointing to his right made signs to me which seemed to say: 'Go this way: have no fear.'

I ran on and on across the rolling plains in the direction he indicated. When evening came I ate a scanty meal of roots and herbs and lay down to rest upon the grass; but fear of the cannibals had robbed me of all desire to sleep, and at midnight I rose again and trudged painfully on.

Thus I journeyed for seven days and nights, and on the morning of the eighth day came at last to the opposite side of the island, where I could faintly discern human figures in the distance. Drawing nearer, I rejoiced to find that they were a party of peasants gathering pepper in a field.

They crowded round me, and speaking in my own language inquired who I was and whence I had come. In reply I recounted the story of my misfortunes, and they were all amazed at my adventure. They congratulated me on my escape and, after offering me food and water, allowed me to rest till evening. When their day's work was done, they took me with them in a boat to their capital, which was in a neighbouring island.

There I was presented to their King, who received me kindly and listened in astonishment to my story. I found their city prosperous and densely populated, abounding in markets and well-stocked shops, and filled with the bustle of commercial activity. The people, both rich and poor, possessed the rarest thoroughbred horses; but I was bewildered to see them ride their steeds bare-backed.

In my next audience with the King I ventured to express my surprise at his subjects' ignorance of the use of saddles and stirrups. 'My noble master,' I remarked, 'why is it that no one in 31 this island uses a saddle? It makes both for the comfort of the rider and his mastery over his horse.'

'What may that be?' he asked, somewhat puzzled. 'I have never seen a saddle in all my life.'

'Pray allow me to make one for you,' I replied, 'that you may try it and find how comfortable and useful it can be.'

The King was pleased at my offer. At once I sought out a skilful carpenter and instructed him to make a wooden frame for a saddle of my own design; then I taught a blacksmith to forge a bit and a pair of stirrups. I fitted out the frame with a padding of wool and leather and furnished it with a girth and tassels. When all was ready, I chose the finest of the royal horses, saddled and bridled it, and led it before the King.

The King was highly delighted with the splendour and usefulness of his horse's novel equipment, and in reward bestowed on me precious gifts and a large sum of money.

When his Vizier saw the saddle he begged me to make one for him. I did so; and it was not long before every courtier and noble in the kingdom became the owner of a handsome saddle.

My skill soon made me the richest man in the island. The King conferred upon me many honours and I became a trusted courtier. One day, as we sat conversing together in his palace, he said: 'You must know, Sindbad, that we have grown to love you like a brother. Indeed, our regard for you is such that we cannot bear the thought that you might some day leave our kingdom. Therefore we will ask you a favour, which we hope you will not refuse.'

'Allah forbid,' I replied, 'that I should refuse you anything, your majesty.'

'We wish you to marry a beautiful girl who has been brought up in our court,' he said. 'She is intelligent and wealthy, and will make you an excellent wife. I trust that you will settle down happily with her in this city for the rest of your days. Do not refuse me this, I pray you.'

I was deeply embarrassed and did not know what to answer.

'Why do you not speak, my son?' he asked.

'Your majesty,' I faltered, 'I am in duty bound to obey you.'

The King sent at once for a cadi and witnesses and I was married that day to a rich woman of noble lineage. The King gave us a magnificent palace and assigned to us a retinue of slaves and servants.

We lived happily and contentedly together, although in my heart of hearts I never ceased to cherish a longing to return home – together with my wife; for I loved her dearly. But, alas, no mortal can control his destiny or trifle with the decrees of Fate.

One day death took my neighbour's wife to eternal rest, and, as he was one of my closest friends, I visited him at his house to offer my condolence. Finding him overcome with grief, I tried to comfort him, saying: 'Have patience, my friend. Allah in His great bounty may soon give you another wife as loving and as worthy as the one He has taken from you. May He lighten your sorrow and prolong your years!'

But he never raised his eyes from the ground.

'Alas!' he sighed. 'How can you wish me a long life when I have but a few hours to live?'

'Take heart, my friend,' I said, 'why do you speak of death when, thank Allah, you are in perfect health, sound in mind and body?'

'In a few hours,' he replied, 'I shall be consigned to the earth with the body of my wife. It is an ancient custom in this country that when a wife dies her husband is buried with her, and if he should die first his wife is buried with him: both must leave this world together.'

'By Allah,' I cried in horror, 'this is a most barbarous custom! No civilized people could ever tolerate such monstrous cruelty!'

Whilst we were talking, my neighbour's friends and kinsfolk, together with a large crowd, came into the house and began to condole with him upon his wife's and his own impending death. Presently the funeral preparations were completed; the woman's body was laid in a coffin, and a long procession of mourners, headed by the husband, formed outside the house. And we all set out towards the burial ground.

The procession halted at the foot of a steep mound overlooking the sea, where a stone was rolled away from the mouth of a deep pit, and into this pit the corpse was thrown. Next the mourners laid hold of my friend and lowered him by a long rope, together with seven loaves of bread and a pitcher of water. Then the stone was rolled back and we all returned to the city.

I hastened with a heavy heart to the King's palace, and when I was admitted to his presence I fell on my knees before him, crying: 'My noble master, I have visited many far countries and lived amongst all manner of men, but in all my life I have never seen or heard of anything so barbarous as your custom of burying the living with the dead. Are strangers, too, subject to this law, your majesty?'

'Certainly they are,' he replied. 'They must be interred with their dead wives. It is a time-hallowed custom to which all must submit.'

At this reply I felt as though my gall-bladder would burst open. I ran in haste to my own house, dreading lest my wife should have died since I last saw her. Finding her in perfect health, I comforted myself as best I could with the thought that I might one day find means of returning to my own country, or even die before my wife.

But Allah ordained otherwise. Soon afterwards my wife was stricken with an illness and in a few days surrendered her soul to the Merciful.

The King and all his courtiers came to my house to comfort me. The body of my wife was perfumed and arrayed in fine robes and rich ornaments. And when all was ready for the burial I was led behind the bier, at the head of a long procession.

When we came to the mound, the stone was lifted from the mouth of the pit and the body of my wife thrown in; then the mourners gathered round to bid me farewell, paying no heed to my protests and entreaties. They bound me with a long rope and lowered me into the pit, together with the customary loaves and pitcher of water. Then they rolled back the stone and went their way.

When I touched the bottom of the pit I found myself in a vast cavern filled with skeletons and reeking with the foul stench of decaying corpses. I threw myself upon the earth, crying: 'You deserve this fate, Sindbad! Here you have come to pay the last penalty for your avarice, your insatiable greed! What need had you to marry in this island? Would that you had died on the bare mountains or perished in the merciless sea!'

Tormented by the vision of a protracted death, I lay in an agony of despair for many hours. At length, feeling the effects of thirst and hunger, I unfastened the loaves and the pitcher of water and ate and drank sparingly. Then I lay in a corner which I had carefully cleared of bones.

For several days I languished in that charnel cave, and at length the time came when my provisions were exhausted. As I lay down, commending myself to Allah and waiting for my approaching end, the covering of the pit was suddenly lifted and there appeared at its mouth a crowd of mourners, who presently lowered into the cavern a dead man accompanied by his screaming wife, together with seven loaves and a pitcher of water.

As soon as the stone was rolled back I rose and, snatching up a leg-bone from one of the skeletons, sprang upon the woman and dealt her a violent blow upon the head, so that she fell down lifeless upon the instant. Then I stole her provisions, which kept me alive for several days longer. When these in turn were finished, the stone was once again rolled away from the pit and a man lowered in with his dead wife. He, too, met the same end as the unfortunate woman before him.

In this way I lived on for many weeks, killing every newcomer and eating his food. One day, as I was sleeping in my accustomed place, I was awakened by a sound of movement near by. At once I sprang to my feet, and picking up my weapon followed the noise until I could faintly discern the form of some animal scurrying before me. As I pressed forward in pursuit of the strange intruder, stumbling in the dark over the bones and corpses, I suddenly made out at the far side of the cavern a tremulous speck of light which grew larger and brighter as I advanced towards it. When I had reached the end of the cave the fleeing animal leapt through the light and disappeared. To my inexpressible joy, I realized that I had come upon a tunnel which the wild beasts, attracted by the carrion in the cave, had burrowed from the other side of the mound. I scrambled into this tunnel, crawling on all fours, and soon found myself at the foot of a high cliff, beneath the open sky.

I fell upon my knees in prayer and thanked the Almighty for my salvation. The warm and wholesome air breathed new life into my veins, and I rejoiced to gaze upon the loveliness of earth and sky.

Fortified with hope and courage, I made my way back into the cave and brought out the store of food which I had laid aside during my sojourn there. I also gathered up all the jewels, pearls, and precious ornaments that I could find upon the corpses, and, tying them in the shrouds and garments of the dead, carried the bundles to the seashore.

I remained there several days, surveying the horizon from morning till night. One day, as I was sitting beneath a rock praying for a speedy rescue, I saw a sail far off upon the ocean. I hoisted a winding-sheet on my staff and waved it frantically as I ran up and down the beach. The crew observed my signal, and a boat was promptly sent off to fetch me.

'How did you find your way to this wild region?' asked the captain in astonishment. 'I have never seen a living man on this desolate spot in all the days of my life.'

'Sir,' I replied, 'I was shipwrecked off this shore many days ago. These bales are the remnants of my goods which I managed to save.' And I kept the truth from him, lest there be some on board who were citizens of that island.

Then I took out a rare pearl from one of my packages and offered it to him. 'Pray accept this,' I said, 'as a token of my gratitude to you for saving my life.'

But the captain politely refused the gift. 'It is not our custom,' he said, 'to accept payment for a good deed. We have rescued many a shipwrecked voyager, fed him and clothed him and finally set him ashore with a little present of our own besides. Allah alone is the giver of rewards.'

I thanked him with all my heart and called down blessings upon him.

Then the ship resumed its voyage. And, as we sailed from island to island and from sea to sea, I rejoiced at the prospect of seeing my native land again. At times, however, a memory of my sojourn with the dead would come back to me and I would be beside myself with terror.

At length, by the grace of Allah, we arrived safely in Basrah. I stayed a few days in that town, and then proceeded up the river to Baghdad. Loaded with treasure, I hastened to my own house, where I was rapturously welcomed by my friends and kinsfolk. I sold for a fabulous sum the precious stones I had brought back from that barbarous city, and gave lavish alms to widows and orphans.

That is the story of my fourth voyage. Tomorrow, if Allah wills, I shall recount to you the adventures of my fifth voyage.

When the evening feast was over, Sindbad the Sailor gave Sindbad the Porter a hundred pieces of gold, and the company took leave of their host and departed, marvelling at all they had heard. Next morning the porter returned, and when the other guests had assembled, Sindbad the Sailor began:

The Fifth Voyage of Sindbad the Sailor

Know, my friends, that the idle and indulgent life which I led after my return soon made me forget the suffering I had endured in the Land of the Cannibals and in the Cavern of the Dead. I remembered only the pleasures of adventure and the considerable gains which my travels had earned me, and once again longed to sail new seas and explore new lands. I equipped myself with commodities suitable for ready sale in foreign countries and, packing them in bales, took them to Basrah.

One day, as I was walking along the wharf, I saw a newly built ship with tall masts and fine new sails which at once caught my fancy. I bought her outright, and embarked in her my slaves and merchandise. Then I hired an experienced captain and a well-trained crew, and accepted as passengers several other merchants who offered to pay their fares beforehand.

Blessed with a favourable wind, we voyaged many days and nights, trading from sea to sea and from shore to shore, and at length came to a desert island where we caught sight of a solitary white dome, half-buried in the sand. This I recognized at once as a roc's egg; and the passengers begged leave to land, so that they might go near and gaze upon this prodigy.

As ill luck would have it, however, the light-hearted merchants found no better sport than to throw great stones at the egg. When the shell was broken, the passengers, who were determined to have a feast, dragged out the young bird and cut it up in pieces. Then they returned on board to tell me of their adventure.

I was filled with horror and cried: 'We are lost! The parent birds will now pursue our ship with implacable rage and destroy us all!'

Scarcely had I finished speaking when the sun was suddenly hidden from our view as by a great cloud and the world grew dark around us as the rocs came flying home. On finding their egg broken and their offspring destroyed, the birds uttered deafening cries; they took to the air again, and in a twinkling vanished from sight.

'All aboard, quickly!' I exclaimed. 'We must at once fly from this island!'

The captain weighed anchor and with all speed we sailed off towards the open sea. But before long the world grew dark again, and in the ominous twilight we could see the gigantic birds hovering high overhead, each carrying in its talons an enormous rock. When they were directly above us, one of them let fall its missile, which narrowly missed the ship and made such a chasm in the ocean that for a moment we could see the sandy bottom. The waves rose mountain-high, tossing us up and down. Presently the other bird dropped its rock, which hit the stern and sent the rudder flying into twenty pieces. Those of us who were not crushed to death were hurled into the sea and swallowed up by the giant waves.

Through the grace of Allah I managed to cling to a floating piece of wreckage. Sitting astride this, I paddled with my feet, and, aided by wind and current, at length reached the shore of an island.

I threw myself upon the sand and lay down awhile to recover my breath. Then I rose and wandered about the island, which was as beautiful as one of the gardens of Eden. The air was filled with the singing of birds, and wherever I turned my eyes I saw trees loaded with luscious fruit and crystal brooks meandering among banks of flowers. I refreshed myself with the fruit and water, and when evening came lay down upon the grass.

Early next morning I rose and set off to explore this solitary garden. After a long stroll among the trees I came to a rivulet where, to my astonishment, I saw, seated upon the bank, a decrepit old man cloaked in a mantle of leaves.

Taking him for a shipwrecked mariner like myself, I went up to him and wished him peace; but he replied only by a mournful nod. I asked him what luckless accident had cast him in that place, but instead of answering he entreated me with signs to take him upon my shoulders and carry him across the brook. I readily bent down and, lifting him upon my back, waded through the stream. When I reached the opposite bank I stooped again for him to get off; but instead of alighting the old wretch powerfully threw his legs, which I now saw were covered with a rough black skin like a buffalo's, round my neck and crossed them tightly over my chest. Seized with fear, I desperately tried to shake him off, but the monster pressed his thighs tighter and tighter round my throat until I could no longer breathe. The world darkened before my eyes and with a choking cry I fell senseless to the ground.

When I came to myself I found the old monster still crouching upon my shoulders, although he had now sufficiently relaxed his hold to allow me to breathe. As soon as he saw that I had recovered my senses he pushed one foot against my belly and, violently kicking my side with the other, forced me to rise and walk under some trees. He leisurely plucked the fruits and ate them, and every time I stopped against his will or failed to do his bidding he kicked me hard, so that I had no choice but to obey him. All day long he remained seated upon my shoulders, 41 and I was no better than a captive slave; at night he made me lie down with him, never for one moment loosening his hold round my neck. Next morning he roused me with a kick and ordered me to carry him among the trees.

Thus he stayed rooted upon my back, discharging his natural filth upon me, and driving me relentlessly on from glade to glade. I cursed the charitable impulse which prompted me to help him, and longed for death to deliver me from my evil plight.

After many weeks of abject servitude I chanced one day to come upon a field where gourds were growing in abundance. Under one of the trees I found a large gourd which was sun-dried and empty. I picked it up and, after cleaning it thoroughly, squeezed into it the juice of several bunches of grapes; then, carefully stopping the hole which I had cut into its shell, left it in the sun to ferment.

When I returned with the old man a few days afterwards, I found the gourd filled with the purest wine. The drink gave me fresh vigour, and I presently began to feel so light and gay that I went tripping merrily among the trees, scarcely aware of my loathsome burden.

Perceiving the effect of the wine, my captor asked me to let him taste it. I did not dare to refuse. He took the gourd from my hand, and raising it to his lips gulped down the liquor to the dregs. When he was overcome with the wine, he began to sway from side to side and his legs gradually relaxed their clasp round my neck. With one violent jerk of my shoulders I hurled him to the ground, where he lay motionless. Then I quickly picked up a great stone from among the trees and, falling upon the old fiend with all my strength, crushed his skull to pieces and mingled his flesh with his blood. That was the end of my tormentor: may Allah have no mercy upon him!

Overjoyed at my new freedom, I roamed the island for many weeks, eating of its fruit and drinking from its springs. One day, however, as I sat on the shore musing on the vicissitudes of my life and recalling memories of my native land, I saw to my great joy a sail heading towards the island. On reaching the beach the vessel anchored, and the passengers went ashore to fill their pitchers with water.

I ran in haste to meet them. They were greatly astonished to see me and gathered round, inquiring who I was and whence I had come. I recounted to them all that had befallen me since my arrival, and they replied: 'It is a marvel that you have escaped from that fiend; for you must know that the monster who had crouched upon your shoulders was none other than the Old Man of the Sea. You are the first ever to escape alive from his clutches. Praise be to Allah for your deliverance!'

They took me to their ship, where the captain received me kindly and listened with astonishment to my adventure. Then we set sail, and after voyaging many days and nights cast anchor in the harbour of a city perched on a high cliff, which is known among travellers as the City of Apes on account of the hosts of monkeys that infest it by night.

I went ashore with one of the merchants from the ship and wandered about the town in search of some employment. We soon fell in with a crowd of men proceeding to the gates of the city with sacks of pebbles on their shoulders. At the sight of these men my friend the merchant gave me a large cotton bag, saying: 'Fill this with pebbles and follow these people into the forest. Do exactly as they do, and thus you will earn your livelihood.'

Following his instructions, I filled the sack with pebbles and joined the crowd. The merchant recommended me to them, 43 saying: 'Here is a shipwrecked stranger; teach him to earn his bread and Allah will reward you.'

When we had marched a great distance from the city we came to a vast valley, covered with coconut-trees so straight and tall that no man could ever climb them. Drawing nearer, I saw among the trees innumerable monkeys, which fled at our approach and swiftly climbed up to the fruit-laden branches.

Here my companions set down their bags and began to pelt the apes with pebbles; and I did the same. The furious beasts retaliated by pelting us with coconuts, and these we gathered up and put into our sacks. When they were full we returned to the city and sold the nuts in the market-place.

Thenceforth I went out every day to the forest with the coconut hunters and traded profitably with the fruit. When I had saved enough money for my homeward voyage I took leave of my friend the merchant and embarked in a vessel bound for Basrah, taking with me a large cargo of coconuts and other produce of that city.

In the course of our voyage we stopped at many heathen islands, where I sold some of my coconuts at a substantial profit and exchanged others for cinnamon, pepper, and Chinese and Comarin aloes. On reaching the Sea of Pearls I engaged the services of several divers; and in a short time brought up a large quantity of priceless pearls.

After that we again set sail and, voyaging many days and nights, at length safely arrived in Basrah. I spent but a few days in that town, and then, loaded with treasure, set out for Baghdad. I rejoiced to be back in my native city, and hastening to my old street, entered my own house, where all my friends and kinsmen forgathered to greet me. I gave them gold and countless presents, and distributed a large sum in charity among the widows and orphans.

That is the story of my fifth voyage. Tomorrow, my friends, if Allah wills, I shall recount to you the tale of my sixth voyage.

When the evening feast was ended, Sindbad the Sailor gave Sindbad the Porter a hundred pieces of gold, and the company departed, marvelling at all they had heard.

Next morning the porter returned and, when the other guests had arrived, Sindbad the Sailor began:

The Sixth Voyage of Sindbad the Sailor

I was one day reclining at my ease in the comfort and felicity of a serene life, when a band of merchants who had just returned from abroad called at my house to give me news of foreign lands. The sight of these travellers recalled to my mind how great was the joy of returning from a far journey to be united with friends and kinsmen after a prolonged absence; and soon afterwards I made preparations for another voyage and set sail with a rich cargo from Basrah.

We voyaged leisurely many days and nights, buying and selling wherever the ship anchored and exploring the unfamiliar places at which we called. One day, however, as we were sailing in mid ocean, we suddenly heard the captain of our ship burst out in a loud lament. He beat himself about the face, tore at his beard, and hurled his turban on the deck. We gathered round him, inquiring the cause of his violent grief.

'Alas, we are lost!' he cried. 'The ship has been driven off its course into an unknown ocean, where nothing can save us from final wreck but Allah's mercy. Let us pray to Him!'

Then, quickly rising, the captain climbed the mast to trim the sails, while the passengers fell on their knees weeping and bidding each other farewell. Scarcely had he reached the top when a violent gale arose, sweeping us swiftly along and dashing the ship against a craggy shore at the foot of a high mountain. At once the vessel split to pieces and we were all flung into the raging sea. Some were drowned outright, while others, like myself, managed to escape by clinging to the jutting rocks.

We found scattered all along the shore the remains of other wrecks, and the sands were strewn with countless bales from which rare merchandise and costly ornaments had broken loose. I wandered among these treasures for many hours, and then, winding my way through the rocks, suddenly came upon a river which flowed from a gorge in the mountain. I followed its course with my eyes and was surprised to find that instead of running into the sea, the river plunged into a vast rocky cavern and disappeared. The banks were covered with glittering jewels, and the bed was studded with myriads of rubies, emeralds, and other precious stones; so that the entire river blazed with a dazzling light. The rarest Chinese and Comarin aloes grew on the adjacent steeps, and liquid amber trickled down the rocks on to the beach below. Great whales would come out of the sea and drink of this amber; but, their bellies being gradually heated, they would at length disgorge it upon the surface of the water. There it would crystallize and, after changing its colour and other properties, would finally be washed ashore, its rich perfume scenting the entire region.

Those of us who had escaped drowning lay in a sorrowful plight upon the shore, counting the days as they dragged by and waiting for the approach of death. One by one my companions died as they came to the end of their provisions, and we who were left washed the dead and wrapped them in winding sheets made from the fabrics scattered on the shore and buried them. Then my friends were stricken with a sickness of the belly, caused by the humid air, to which they all succumbed; and I had the melancholy task of burying with my own hands the last of my companions.

Realizing that death was at hand, I threw myself upon the earth, wailing: 'Would that I had died before my friends! There would at least have remained good comrades who would have washed my body and given it a decent burial! There is no strength or help save in Allah!'

At length I rose and dug a deep grave by the sea, thinking to myself: 'When I sense the approach of death I will lie here and die in my grave. In time the wind will bury me with sand.' And as I thus prepared to meet my end, I cursed myself for venturing yet again upon the perils of the sea after having suffered so many misfortunes in my past voyages. 'Why,' I cried in my despair, 'O why were you not content to remain safe and happy in Baghdad? Had you not enough riches to last you twice a lifetime?'

Lost in these reflections, I wandered to the banks of the river, and as I watched it disappear into the cavern I struck upon a plan. 'By Allah,' I thought, 'this river must have both a beginning and an end. If it enters the mountain on this side it must surely emerge into daylight again; and if I can but follow its course in some vessel, the current may at last bring me to some inhabited land. If I am destined to survive this peril, Allah will guide me to safety; if I perish, it will not be worse than the dismal fate which awaits me here.'

Emboldened by these thoughts, I collected some large branches of Chinese and Comarin aloes and, laying these on some planks from the wrecked vessels, bound them with strong cables into a raft. This I loaded with sacks of rubies, pearls, and other stones, as well as several bales of the choicest ambergris; then, commending myself to Allah, I launched the raft upon the water and jumped aboard.

The current carried me swiftly along, and I soon found myself enveloped in the brooding darkness of the cavern. My raft began to bump violently against the ragged sides, while the passage grew smaller and narrower until I was compelled to lie flat upon my belly for fear of striking my head. Very soon I wished I could return to the open shore, but the current became faster and faster as the river swept headlong down its precipitous bed, and I resigned myself to certain death. At length, overcome by terror and exertion, I sank into a death-like sleep.

I cannot tell how long I slept, but when I awoke I found myself lying on my raft close to the river bank, beneath the open sky. The river was flowing gently through a stretch of pleasant meadowland, and on the bank stood many Indians and Abyssinians.

As soon as these men saw that I was awake, they gathered about me, asking questions in a language I did not understand. Presently one of their number came forward and greeted me in Arabic.

'Who may you be?' he asked, 'and whence have you come? We were working in our fields when we saw you drifting down the river. We fastened your raft to this bank and, not wishing to disturb your slumbers, left you here in safety. But tell us, what accident has cast you upon this river, which takes its perilous course from beneath that mountain?'

I begged him first to give me some food, and promised to answer all their questions after I had eaten. They instantly brought me a variety of meats, and when I had regained my strength a little, I recounted to them all that had befallen me since my shipwreck. They marvelled at my miraculous escape, and said: 'We must take you to our King, so that you may yourself tell him of your adventure.'

Thereupon they led me to their city, carrying my raft with all its contents upon their shoulders. The King received me courteously and, after listening in profound astonishment to my story, congratulated me heartily on my escape. Then, opening my treasures in his presence, I laid out at his feet a priceless choice of emeralds, pearls, and rubies. In return he conferred upon me the highest honours of the kingdom, and invited me to stay as his guest at the palace.

Thus I rose rapidly in the King's favour, and soon became a trusted courtier. One day he questioned me about my country and its far-famed Caliph. I praised the wisdom, piety, and benevolence of Haroun Al-Rashid, and spoke at length of his glorious deeds. The King was profoundly impressed by my account. 'This monarch,' he said, 'must indeed be illustrious. We desire to send him a present worthy of his greatness, and appoint you the bearer of it.'

'I hear and obey,' I replied. 'I will gladly deliver your gift to the Prince of the Faithful, and will inform him that in your majesty he has a worthy ally and a trusted friend.'

The King gave orders that a magnificent present be prepared and commissioned a new vessel for the voyage. When all was ready for departure I presented myself at the royal palace and, thanking the King for the many favours he had shown me, took leave of him and of the officers of his court.

Then I set sail, and voyaging many days and nights at length safely arrived in Basrah. I hastened to Baghdad with the royal gift, and when I had been admitted to the Caliph's presence I kissed the ground before him and told him of my mission. Al-Rashid marvelled greatly at my adventure and gave orders that the story be inscribed on parchment in letters of gold, so that it might be preserved among the treasures of the kingdom.

Leaving his court, I hastened to my old street and, entering my own house, rejoiced to meet my friends and kinsfolk. I gave them gold and costly presents, and distributed lavish alms among the poor of the city.

Such is the story of my sixth voyage. Tomorrow, my friends, I shall recount to you the tale of my seventh and last voyage.

When the evening feast was ended, Sindbad the Sailor gave Sindbad the Porter a hundred pieces of gold, and the guests departed, marvelling at all they had heard.

Next morning the porter returned and, when the other guests had assembled, Sindbad the Sailor began:

The Last Voyage of Sindbad the Sailor

For many years after my return I lived joyfully in Baghdad, feasting and carousing with my boon companions and revelling away the riches which my farflung travels had earned me. But though I was now past the prime of life, my untamed spirit rebelled against my declining years, and I once again longed to see the world and travel in the lands of men. I made preparations for a long voyage and, boarding a good ship in company with some eminent merchants, set sail from Basrah with a fair wind and a rich cargo.

We voyaged peacefully for many weeks, but one day, whilst we were sailing in the China Sea, a violent tempest struck our ship, drenching us with torrents of rain. We hastily covered our bales with canvas to protect them from the wet and fervently prayed to Allah to save us from the fury of the sea, while the captain, rolling up his sleeves and tucking the skirts of his robes into his belt, climbed the mast and from the top scanned the horizon in all directions. Presently he climbed down again, all in a tremble with terror and, staring at us with an expression of blank despair, beat his face and plucked the hairs of his beard.

'Pray to Allah,' he cried, 'that He may save us from the peril into which we have fallen! Weep and say your farewells, for the treacherous wind has got the better of us and driven our ship into the world's farthermost ocean!'

Thereupon the captain opened one of his cabin chests and took from it a small cotton bag filled with an ashlike powder. He sprinkled some water over the powder and, after waiting a little, inhaled it into his nostrils; then, opening a little book, he intoned aloud some strange incantations and at length turned to us, crying: 'Know that we are now approaching the Realm of Kings, the very land where our master Solomon son of David (may peace be upon him) lies buried. Serpents of prodigious size swarm about that coast, and the sea is filled with giant whales which can swallow vessels whole. Farewell, my friends; and may Allah have mercy upon us all!'

Scarcely had the captain uttered these words when suddenly the ship was tossed high up in the air and then flung down into the sea, while an ear-splitting cry, more terrible than thunder, boomed through the swelling ocean. Terror seized our hearts as we saw a gigantic whale, as massive as a mountain, rushing swiftly towards us, followed by another no less huge, and a third greater than the two put together. This last monster bounded from the surging billows and, opening wide its enormous mouth, seized in its jaws the ship with all that was in it. I hastily ran to the edge of the tilting deck and, casting off my clothes, leapt into the sea just before the whale swallowed up the ship and disappeared beneath the foam with its two companions.

With Allah's help I clung to a piece of timber which had fallen from the lost vessel and, contending with the mighty waves for two days and nights, was at length cast on an island covered with fruit-trees and watered by many streams. After refreshing myself I wandered aimlessly about, and soon came to a fast-flowing river which rolled its waters towards the interior of the island. As I stood upon the bank I hit upon the idea of building a raft and allowing myself to be carried down by the current, as I had done in my last voyage. 'If I succeed in saving myself this time,' I said, 'all will be well with me and I solemnly vow never in all my life to let the mere thought of voyaging cross my mind again. If I fail, I shall at last find rest from all the toils and tribulations which my incorrigible folly has earned me.'

I cut down several branches from an exotic tree which I had never seen before and bound them together into a raft with the stems of some creeping plants. I loaded the raft with a large quantity of fruit and, commending myself to Allah, pushed off down the river.

For three days and nights I was hurried swiftly along by the current, until, overcome by dizziness, I sank into a dead faint. When I recovered consciousness I found myself heading towards a fearful precipice, down which the waters of the river were tumbling in a mighty cataract. I clung with all my strength to the branches of the raft and, resigning myself to my fate, prayed silently for a merciful end. When I had reached the very edge of the precipice, however, I suddenly felt the raft halted upon the water and found myself caught in a net which a crowd of men had thrown from the bank. My raft was quickly hauled to land, and I was released from the net half dead with terror and exhaustion.

As I lay upon the mud, I gradually became aware of a venerable old man who was bending over me. He wrapped me in warm garments and greeted me kindly; and when my strength had returned a little he helped me to rise and led me slowly to the baths of the city, where I was washed with perfumed water. Then the old man took me to his own house. He regaled me sumptuously with excellent meats and wines and, when the feast was ended, his slaves washed my hands and wiped them with napkins of the rarest silk. After this my host conducted me to a noble chamber and left me alone, after assigning several of his slaves to my service.

The kind old man entertained me in this fashion for three

days. When I had completely recovered, he visited me in my chamber and sat conversing with me for an hour. Just before leaving my room, however, he turned to me and said: 'If you wish to sell your merchandise, my friend, I will gladly come down with you to the market-place.'

I was greatly puzzled at these words and did not know what to answer, as I had been cast utterly naked in that city.

'Do not be troubled over your goods, my son,' went on the old man. 'If we receive a good offer, we will sell them outright; if not, I will keep them for you in my own storehouse until they fetch a better price.'

Concealing my perplexity, I replied: 'I am willing to do whatever you advise.' With this I rose and went out with him to the market-place.

There I saw an excited crowd admiring an object on the ground with exclamations of enthusiastic praise. Pushing my way among the gesticulating merchants, I was astonished to find the centre of attention to be no other than the raft aboard which I had sailed down the river. And presently the old man ordered a broker to begin the auction.

'Who will make the first bid for this rare sandalwood?' began the broker.

'A hundred dinars!' cried one of the merchants.

'A thousand!' shouted another.

'Eleven hundred!' exclaimed my host.

'Agreed!' I cried.

Upon this the old man ordered his slaves to carry the wood to his store and walked back with me to his house,, where he paid me eleven hundred pieces of gold locked in an iron coffer.

One day, as we sat conversing together, the old man said: 'My son, pray grant me a favour.'

'With all my heart,' I replied.

'I am a very old man, and have not been blessed with a son,' went on my benefactor. 'Yet I have a young and beautiful daughter, who on my death will be sole mistress of my fortune. If you will have her for your wife, you will inherit my wealth and become chief of the merchants of this city.'

I readily consented to the sheikh's proposal. A sumptuous feast was held, a cadi and witnesses were called in, and I was married to the old man's daughter amidst great rejoicings. When the wedding guests had departed I was conducted to the bridal chamber, where I was allowed to see my wife for the first time. I found her incomparably beautiful, and rejoiced to see her decked with the rarest pearls and jewels.

My wife and I grew to love each other dearly, and we lived together in happiness and contentment. Not long afterwards my wife's father died, and I inherited all his possessions. His slaves became my slaves and his goods my goods, and the merchants of the city appointed me their chief in his place.

One day, however, I discovered that every year the people of that land experienced a wondrous change in their bodies. All the men grew wings upon their shoulders and for a whole day flew high up in the air, leaving their wives and children behind. Amazed at this prodigy, I importuned one of my friends to allow me to cling to him when he next took his flight, and at length prevailed on him to let me try this novel adventure. When the long-awaited day arrived, I took tight hold of my friend's waist and was at once carried up swiftly in the air. We climbed higher and higher into the void until I could hear the angels in their choirs singing hymns to Allah under the vault of heaven. Moved with awe, I cried: 'Glory and praise eternal be to Allah, King of the Universe!'

Scarcely had I uttered these words when my winged carrier dropped headlong through the air and finally alighted on the top of a high mountain. There he threw me off his back and took to the air again, calling down curses on my head. Abandoned upon this desolate mountain, I lifted my hands in despair and cried: 'There is no strength or help save in Allah! Every time I escape from one ordeal I find myself in another as grievous. Surely I deserve all that befalls me!'

Whilst I was thus reflecting upon my plight, I saw two youths coming up towards me. Their faces shone with an unearthly beauty, and each held a staff of red gold in his hand. I at once rose to my feet, and, walking towards them, wished them peace. They returned my greeting courteously, and I inquired: 'Who are you, pray, and what object has brought you to this barren mountain?'

'We are worshippers of the True God,' they replied. With this, one of the youths pointed to a certain path upon the mountain and, handing me his staff, walked away with his companion.

Bewildered at these words, I set off in the direction he had indicated, leaning upon my gold staff as I walked. I had not gone far when I saw coming towards me the flyer who had so unceremoniously set me down upon the mountain. Determined to learn the reason of his displeasure, I went up to him and said gently: 'Is this how friends behave to friends?'

The winged man, who was now no longer angry, replied: 'Know that my fall was caused by your unfortunate mention of your god. The word has this effect upon us all, and this is why we never utter it.'

I assured my friend that I had meant no harm and promised to commit no such transgression in future. Then I begged him to carry me back to the city. He took me upon his shoulders and in a few moments set me down before my own house.

My wife was overjoyed at my return, and when I told her of my adventure, she said: 'We must no longer stay among these people. Know that they are the brothers of Satan and have no knowledge of the True God.'

'How then did your father dwell amongst them?' I asked.

'My father was of an alien race,' she replied. 'He shared none of their creeds, and he did not lead their life. As he is now dead, let us sell our possessions and leave this blasphemous city.'

Thereupon I resolved to return home. We sold our houses and other property, and hiring a vessel set sail with a rich cargo.

Aided by a favouring wind, we voyaged many days and nights and at length came to Basrah and thence to Baghdad, the City of Peace. I conveyed to my stores the valuables I had brought with me, and, taking my wife to my own house in my old street, rejoiced to meet my kinsfolk and my old companions. They told me that this voyage had kept me abroad for nearly twenty-seven years, and marvelled exceedingly at all that had befallen me.

I rendered deep thanks to Allah for bringing me safely back to my friends and kinsfolk, and solemnly vowed never to travel again by sea or land. Such, dear guests, was the last and longest of my voyages.

When the evening feast was ended, Sindbad the Sailor gave Sindbad the Porter a hundred pieces of gold, which he took with thanks and blessings and departed, marvelling at all he had heard.

The porter remained a constant visitor at the house of his illustrious friend, and the two lived in amity and peace until there came to them the Spoiler of worldly mansions, the Dark Steward of the graveyard; the Shadow which dissolves the bonds of friendship and ends alike all joys and all sorrows.

PENGUIN 60s

MARTIN AMIS · *God's Dice*

HANS CHRISTIAN ANDERSEN · *The Emperor's New Clothes*

MARCUS AURELIUS · *Meditations*

JAMES BALDWIN · *Sonny's Blues*

AMBROSE BIERCE · *An Occurrence at Owl Creek Bridge*

DIRK BOGARDE · *From Le Pigeonnier*

WILLIAM BOYD · *Killing Lizards*

POPPY Z. BRITE · *His Mouth will Taste of Wormwood*

ITALO CALVINO · *Ten Italian Folktales*

ALBERT CAMUS · *Summer*

TRUMAN CAPOTE · *First and Last*

RAYMOND CHANDLER · *Goldfish*

ANTON CHEKHOV · *The Black Monk*

ROALD DAHL · *Lamb to the Slaughter*

ELIZABETH DAVID · *I'll be with You in the Squeezing of a Lemon*

N. J. DAWOOD (TRANS.) · *The Seven Voyages of Sindbad the Sailor*

ISAK DINESEN · *The Dreaming Child*

SIR ARTHUR CONAN DOYLE · *The Man with the Twisted Lip*

DICK FRANCIS · *Racing Classics*

SIGMUND FREUD · *Five Lectures on Psycho-Analysis*

KAHLIL GIBRAN · *Prophet, Madman, Wanderer*

STEPHEN JAY GOULD · *Adam's Navel*

ALASDAIR GRAY · *Five Letters from an Eastern Empire*

GRAHAM GREENE · *Under the Garden*

JAMES HERRIOT · *Seven Yorkshire Tales*

PATRICIA HIGHSMITH · *Little Tales of Misogyny*

M. R. JAMES AND R. L. STEVENSON · *The Haunted Dolls' House*

RUDYARD KIPLING · *Baa Baa, Black Sheep*

PENELOPE LIVELY · *A Long Night at Abu Simbel*

KATHERINE MANSFIELD · *The Escape*

PENGUIN 60s

GABRIEL GARCÍA MÁRQUEZ · *Bon Voyage, Mr President*
PATRICK MCGRATH · *The Angel*
HERMAN MELVILLE · *Bartleby*
SPIKE MILLIGAN · *Gunner Milligan, 954021*
MICHEL DE MONTAIGNE · *Four Essays*
JAN MORRIS · *From the Four Corners*
JOHN MORTIMER · *Rumpole and the Younger Generation*
R. K. NARAYAN · *Tales from Malgudi*
ANAIS NIN · *A Model*
FRANK O'CONNOR · *The Genius*
GEORGE ORWELL · *Pages from a Scullion's Diary*
CAMILLE PAGLIA · *Sex and Violence, or Nature and Art*
SARA PARETSKY · *A Taste of Life*
EDGAR ALLAN POE · *The Pit and the Pendulum*
MISS READ · *Village Christmas*
JEAN RHYS · *Let Them Call It Jazz*
DAMON RUNYON · *The Snatching of Bookie Bob*
SAKI · *The Secret Sin of Septimus Brope*
WILL SELF · *Scale*
GEORGES SIMENON · *Death of a Nobody*
MURIEL SPARK · *The Portobello Road*
ROBERT LOUIS STEVENSON · *The Pavilion on the Links*
PAUL THEROUX · *Down the Yangtze*
WILLIAM TREVOR · *Matilda's England*
MARK TULLY · *Ram Chander's Story*
JOHN UPDIKE · *Friends from Philadelphia*
EUDORA WELTY · *Why I Live at the P. O.*
EDITH WHARTON · *Madame de Treymes*
OSCAR WILDE · *The Happy Prince*
VIRGINIA WOOLF · *Killing the Angel in the House*

For complete information about books available from Penguin and how to order them, please write to us at the appropriate address below. Please note that for copyright reasons the selection of books varies from country to country.

IN THE UNITED KINGDOM: Please write to *Dept. JC, Penguin Books Ltd, FREEPOST, West Drayton, Middlesex UB7 OBR.*
If you have any difficulty in obtaining a title, please send your order with the correct money, plus ten per cent for postage and packaging, to *PO Box No. 11, West Drayton, Middlesex UB7 OBR.*

IN THE UNITED STATES: Please write to *Consumer Sales, Penguin USA, P.O. Box 999, Dept. 17109, Bergenfield, New Jersey 07621-0120.* VISA and MasterCard holders call 1-800-253-6476 to order all Penguin titles.

IN CANADA: Please write to *Penguin Books Canada Ltd, 10 Alcorn Avenue, Suite 300, Toronto, Ontario M4V 3B2.*

IN AUSTRALIA: Please write to *Penguin Books Australia Ltd, P.O. Box 257, Ringwood, Victoria 3134.*

IN NEW ZEALAND: Please write to *Penguin Books (NZ) Ltd, Private Bag 102902, North Shore Mail Centre, Auckland 10.*

IN INDIA: Please write to *Penguin Books India Pvt Ltd, 706 Eros Apartments, 56 Nehru Place, New Delhi 110 019.*

IN THE NETHERLANDS: Please write to *Penguin Books Netherlands bv, Postbus 3507, NL-1001 AH Amsterdam.*

IN GERMANY: Please write to *Penguin Books Deutschland GmbH, Metzlerstrasse 26, 60594 Frankfurt am Main.*

IN SPAIN: Please write to *Penguin Books S. A., Bravo Murillo 19, 1o B, 28015 Madrid.*

IN ITALY: Please write to *Penguin Italia s.r.l., Via Felice Casati 20, I-20124 Milano.*

IN FRANCE: Please write to *Penguin France S. A., 17 rue Lejeune, F-31000 Toulouse.*

IN JAPAN: Please write to *Penguin Books Japan, Ishikiribashi Building, 2-5-4, Suido, Bunkyo-ku, Tokyo 112.*

IN GREECE: Please write to *Penguin Hellas Ltd, Dimocritou 3, GR-106 71 Athens.*

IN SOUTH AFRICA: Please write to *Longman Penguin Southern Africa (Pty) Ltd, Private Bag X08, Bertsham 2013.*